D0418797

For Barbara, who makes bears
S.H.

For Edward (Teddy) Craig
H.C.

First published 1986 by Walker Books Ltd
87 Vauxhall Walk, London SE11 5HJ

This edition published 1992

Text © 1986 Sarah Hayes
Illustrations © 1986 Helen Craig

Printed and bound in Singapore by
Tien Wah Press (Pte.) Ltd

British Library Cataloguing in Publication Data
A catalogue record for this book is available
from the British Library.
ISBN 0-7445-2539-X

— THIS IS THE —
BEAR

WRITTEN BY
Sarah Hayes

ILLUSTRATED BY
Helen Craig

WALKER BOOKS
LONDON

This is the bear
who fell in the bin.

This is the dog
who pushed him in.

This is the man
who picked up the sack.

This is the driver
who would not come back.

This is the bear

who went to the dump

and fell on the pile
with a bit of a bump.

This is the boy

who took the bus

and went to the dump
to make a fuss.

This is the man
in an awful grump
who searched

and searched
and searched the dump.

This is the bear
all cold and cross

who did not think
he was really lost.

This is the dog

who smelled the smell

of a bone

and a tin

and a bear as well.

This is the man
who drove them home –

the boy, the bear
and the dog with a bone.

This is the bear
all lovely and clean

who did not say

just where he had been.

This is the boy
who knew quite well,

but promised his friend
he would not tell.

And this is the boy
who woke up in the night
and asked the bear
if he felt all right –
and was very surprised
when the bear shouted out,
'How soon can we have
another day out?'